AUSTIN MANNING

ILLUSTRATED
BY
SEAN MICHAEL VALENTIN

INKED & COLORED
BY
SEAN MICHAEL VALENTIN

WRITTEN
BY
SEAN MICHAEL VALENTIN

CHARACTERS CREATED
AND
DESIGNED
BY
SEAN MICHAEL VALENTIN

FOLLOW ME
ON
TWITTER AND BLUESKY!
@DARKVICEV
FOR UPDATES AND NEW RELEASES!

SEAN MICHAEL VALENTIN

PRESENTS

WELCOME
TO
PHANTOM
FALLS™

NO. 4

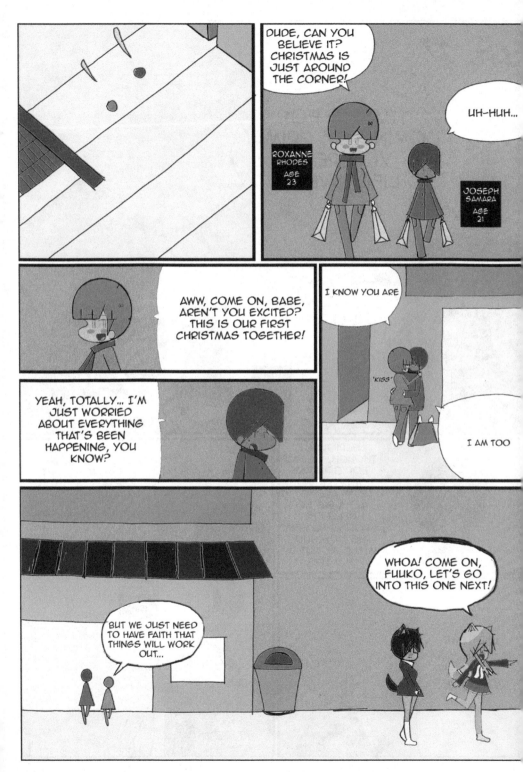

LOOK AT ALL THIS STUFF! WE'LL DEFINITELY FIND SOME GOOD PRESENTS IN HERE!

I HAVE A FEELING YOU'RE RIGHT, LADY MAKURO... I'M EXCITED TO FINALLY MEET EVERYONE. I HOPE WE CAN FIND SOMETHING NICE FOR THE LITTLE ONES

FUUKO FUJIMORI
AGE 20

OH, WOW! THESE ARE PERFECT!
-MAKURO-

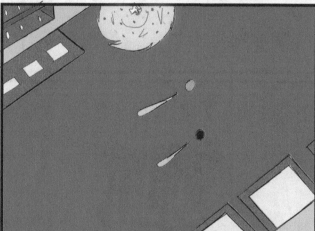

CHECK 'EM OUT, AREN'T THESE GREAT!

VERY CUTE...

THANK YOU FOR YOUR BUSINESS. WE LOOK FORWARD TO YOUR NEXT VISIT!

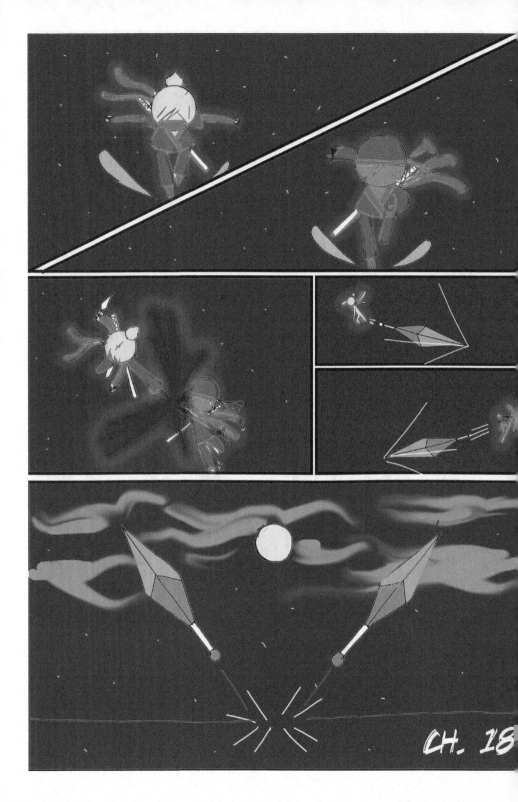

CH. 18

DAMN... GOOD TO SEE YOU'RE AS SHARP AS EVER

KAI
AGE
42

SHARP ENOUGH TO TAKE DOWN THE BIG GUY?

SADLY, I'M NOT SURE, PERHAPS MOMENTARILY, BUT IT'S FAR TOO CLOSE TO SAY IF YOU COULD PUT HIM DOWN FOR GOOD

HIRO
FUJIMORI
AGE
43

CRAP... I WAS AFRAID OF THAT... BY THE WAY... I GOT SOME NEWS FROM MY MOLE AND APPARENTLY... OUR ENEMY HAS SOMETHING BIG PLANNED... ONE LAST STAND OFF TO FINALLY END THIS BACK AND FORTH OF OURS... SET FOR DECEMBER 31ST

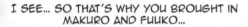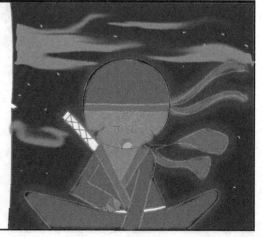

I SEE... SO THAT'S WHY YOU BROUGHT IN MAKURO AND FUUKO...

SO, THE DOG STAYED HOME, HUH? WHAT A LITTLE BITCH

PLEASE, THE R DESERVES IT FC KNOCKING ME HALFWAY ACROSS THE CITY...

HITOMI FUJIMORI

AGE 20

A FEW MONTHS OLDER THEN MIDC

I MEAN, CAN YOU BLAME HIM? YOU MADE QUITE THE IMPRESSION

I APPRECIATE IT, BUT IT'S NOT YOUR FAULT THAT THE MUTT IS SNEAKY

AGAIN, I'M REALLY SORRY ABOUT THAT...

BY THE WAY, HAVE YOU DONE ANY CHRISTMAS SHOPPING YET?

10

UH-HUH, I DID ALL OF MINE ON BLACK FRIDAY! IT WAS A BLAST...

THINKING OF ALL THE FIGHTING SHE DID

WHY AM I NOT SURPRISED...

BY THE WAY, YOU GUYS ARE GOING TO MIRANDA'S TO HELP FINISH UP THE DECORATING, RIGHT? YOU GUYS SHOULD JUST SPEND THE NIGHT!

SURE, WE CAN ALL HEAD OVER IN THE MORNING

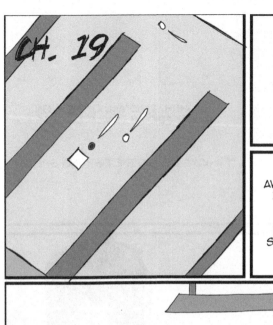

CH. 19

I CAN'T BELIEVE MASTER KAI IS LETTING THOSE GIRLS MOVE IN WITH US...

AWW, COME ON, I KINDA LIKE 'EM... THAT MAKURO ESPECIALLY, SHE'S FUNNY...

THAT'S NOT THE POINT... THE PLACE IS TOO SMALL FOR 5 PEOPLE... PLUS, THEY HAVE THE APPETITE OF AN ELEPHANT...

WELL, I SUPPOSE I'LL HAVE TO AGREE WITH THAT LAST PART

LEE
AGE
18

GOT THE LAST CAN

OH HEY... ISN'T T GIRL ONE OF RADAMS' FRIENC MAYBE WE SHOL INTRODUCE OURSELVES?
-LEE

SORRY, BUT I'M GONNA HAVE TO PASS ON THAT ONE, CHIEF. I'LL SEE YA AT HOME

NO SURPRISE THERE

ZERA
~
SHORIN
AGE
18

HI... YOU'RE FRIENDS WITH RADAMS, RIGHT? I'M LEE

YUP!

THAT'S RIGHT! I'M MIRANDA, IT'S NICE TO MEET YOU! YOU MUST BE HIS FRIEND TOO, RIGHT?!

AWESOME! BY THE WAY, I'M PLANNING ON HAVING A SMALL GET-TOGETHER WITH SOME FRIENDS OF MINE FOR CHRISTMAS... I WOULD LOVE IT IF YOU CAME!

FOR SURE! SOUNDS LIKE FUN... I'LL BE THERE
-LEE-

MMMM... THAT SMELLS SO GOOD! THANK YOU FOR COOKING FOR US, MIRANDA! YOU'RE THE BEST!

AWW, OF COURSE, DEAR! AFTER ALL, YOU GUYS HAVE BEEN A MASSIVE HELP THIS WEEK WITH ALL THE DECORATING, IT'S THE LEAST I COULD DO...

BUT SERIOUSLY, MY MOUTH IS WATERING, JUST THINKING ABOUT EATING ONE OF YOUR DISHES!

SPEAKING OF DECORATING, COULD YOU CHECK UP ON THE OTHERS AND SEE HOW THEY'RE DOING?

SPENCER

AGE 8

WW, HITOMI! YOU REALLY ARE UCH A SWEETIE! THANK YOU!

SURE -HITOMI-

HEY, ARE YOU GUYS ALMOST DONE?

KILLER SHOW AS ALWAYS, VICTORIA, YOU SOMEHOW MANAGED TO OUTDO YOURSELF ONCE AGAIN!

JASON KWON AGE 24

AWW, THANKS, BUDDY, BUT I REALLY DON'T DESERVE ALL OF YOUR PRAISE! I'M MERELY A HUMBLE BEAUTY...

VICTORIA ROBIN AGE 21

YEAH, TOTALLY HUMBLE! ANYWAY, WHAT ARE YOUR HOLIDAY PLANS?

NOAH SIMPSON AGE 24

WELL, MIRANDA'S THROWING THIS LITTLE CHRISTMAS SHINDIG, SO I WAS PLANNING ON GOING TO THAT... PLUS, CODY'S OUT OF TOWN VISITING HIS FOLKS... YOU LOOKING TO JOIN ME? –VICTORIA–

CAN'T, I HAVE WORK...

DUDE, ARE THEY SERIOUSLY MAKING YOU WORK THE HOLIDAYS?!

EH, I'M USED TO IT! SUCH ARE THE PITFALLS OF FOOD SERVICE... AAAND CAPITALISM

CH. 20

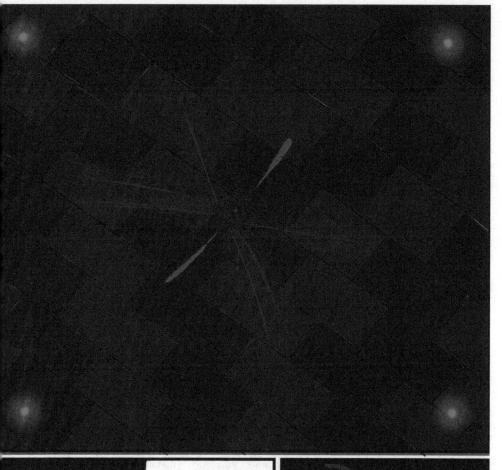

TELL ME, DID YOU REALLY THINK YOU COULD JUST LEAVE THE GROUP... WITHOUT HAVING TO FIGHT YOUR WAY OUT?!

PLEASE, ONE WOULD HAVE TO BE FOOL TO ASSUME OTHERWISE

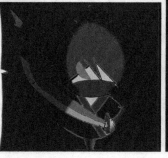

AS ALWAYS... SPOKEN LIKE A TRUE WARRIOR! FUJIMORI... SANOSUKE-SAN!!!

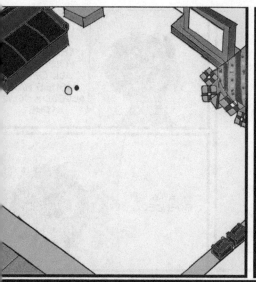

AWW, LOOK AT YOU!

ARE YOU EXCITED FOR CHRISTMAS, SWEETIE PIE?!

ARE YOU EXCITED TO PLAY WITH ALL YOUR NEW TOYS?!

YEA!

YEA!!!!!!!

LOOKS LIKE SOMEONE DECIDED TO TAKE A BIT OF A NAP, HUH?

ZETSUBOU

AGE UNKNOWN

YOU LET HIM ESCAPE

YUP, WHILE IT IS TRUE THAT HE IS PRETTY TOUGH, HE CAN STILL GET STRONGER

HERE... I FIGURED YOU MIGHT WANT A CHANGE OF CLOTHES
-ZETSUBOU-

OH, WOW! THANKS... I APPRECIATE IT!

YOU KNOW SOMETHING, YOU'RE A PRETTY GOOD GUY, ALL THINGS CONSIDERED!

WHILE IT IS TRUE THAT MOST OF US HAVE KNOWN EACH OTHER FOR QUITE SOME TIME NOW...
-MIDORI-

...OUR FRIEND GROUP HAS ALWAYS SEEMED... SORT OF FRAGMENTED...
-MIDORI-

...AND BECAUSE OF THAT, I ALWAYS FELT A BIT OF INDIFFERENCE...
-MIDORI-

...BUT EVERYTHING FEELS DIFFERENT NOW...
-MIDORI-

...THERE'S A SENSE OF WARMTH THAT I HAVEN'T FELT BEFORE!
-MIDORI-

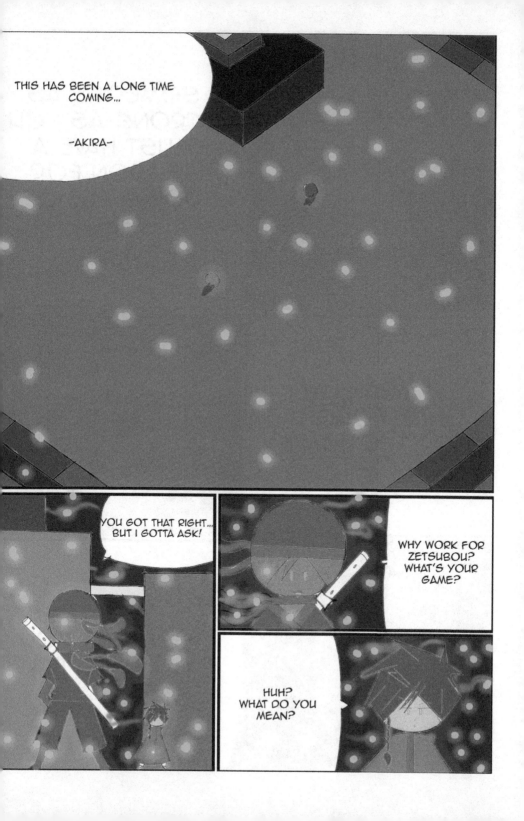

SOMEONE AS STRONG AS YOU MUST HAVE A REASON FOR DOING ALL OF THIS...
-KAI-

...I MEAN, WE ONCE FOUGHT FOR THE SAME SIDE...

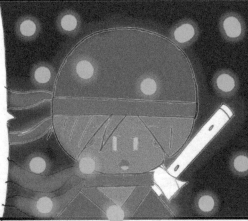

...SO TELL ME... WHY HAVE YOU FALLEN SO FAR?

-KAI-

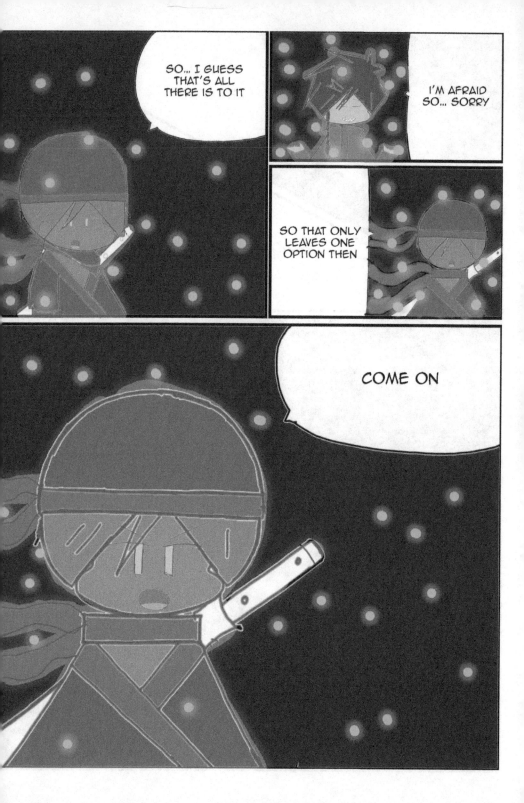

DAMN IT... THINGS HAVE ALREADY STARTED...
-SANOSUKE-

...AND I STILL HAVE A WAYS TO GO!
-SANOSUKE-

HANG ON TIGHT, HITOMI...
-SANOSUKE-

...I'M ON MY WAY!!!
-SANOSUKE-

EDITORS
-
ROBERTA
ADAMS

ILLUSTRATED
BY
SEAN MICHAEL VALENTIN

INKED & COLORED
BY
SEAN MICHAEL VALENTIN

WRITTEN
BY
SEAN MICHAEL VALENTIN

CHARACTERS CREATED
AND
DESIGNED
BY
SEAN MICHAEL VALENTIN

FOLLOW ME
ON
TWITTER AND BLUESKY!
@DARKVICEV
FOR UPDATES AND NEW RELEASES!

SEAN MICHAEL VALENTIN

PRESENTS

WELCOME
To
PHANTOM
FALLS™

NO. 5

SO...
-AKIRA-

...WHATCHA NEED ME TO DO?
-AKIRA-

NOTHING MUCH... JUST KEEP KAI BUSY FOR ME, WHILE I PUT THE LAST PIECES OF MY COUNTER STRATEGY IN PLACE

YOU SURE ABOUT THAT? SEEMS SORTA RISKY

SCARED? NEVER. I'LL GET IT DONE

HUH? YOU'RE NOT SCARED, ARE YA?
-HIRO-

IF I DON'T FIND A WAY
OUT OF THIS MESS...
-AKIRA-

...THIS COULD GET
REALLY... REALLY...
-AKIRA-

...DANGEROUS...
-AKIRA-

...I GOTTA END THIS... NOW!
-AKIRA-

SO, HOW DO YOU THINK THE OTHERS ARE DOING?

CONSIDERING HOW CRAZY THINGS HAVE GOTTEN AROUND HERE...

WELL, CRAZIER, BUT I GET WHAT YOU'RE SAYING... I'M SURE THEY'RE FINE

BY THE WAY, I WONDER WHAT THAT ARASHI GUY IS UP TO. THINK WE'LL SEE HIM AGAIN?

WHO KNOWS...

SO LET ME GET THIS STRAIGHT... YOU'RE NOT... ONE OF ZETSUBOU'S GUYS... -LEE-

...RIGHT?

CORRECT...

COOL, BUT THAT STILL DOESN'T EXPLAIN WHY YOU ATTACKED ME?

AN ASSUMPTION ON MY PART... GIVEN HOW POWERFUL YOUR SPIRITUAL RESIDUALS ARE, I ASSUMED THE WORST... PLEASE ACCEPT MY APOLOGIES.

EH, IT'S WHATEVER

AT LEAST WE'RE ALL ON THE SAME PAGE NOW, RIGHT?

CH. 24

HEY, ROXY, CAN YOU DO ME A FAVOR?

SURE, WHAT'S UP?

OKIE DOKIE... LEAVE IT TO ME!

WOULD YOU MIND GOING UPSTAIRS AND BRINGING SPENCER SOME FOOD? IT'S BEEN A FEW HOURS, AND I'M SURE THE CUTIE MUST BE HUNGRY...

YO! SPENCE, IT'S CHOW TIME! SO, I'M COMING IN, ALRIGHT?!

REST EASY, MY FRIEND
-ZETSUBOU-

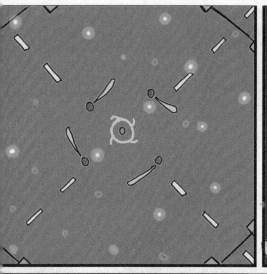

DAMN IT!
-RADAMS-

O MATTER HOW
ARD I STRIKE AT
HIM!
-RADAMS-

THAT WATER OF HIS... WILL JUST KEEP BLOCKING MY PATH... IT'S IMPOSSIBLE!
-RADAMS-

WELL... WELL... IT SEEMS LIKE YOU'RE FINALLY FIGURING IT OUT!

SO ALLOW ME TO EXPLAIN...
-J-

INCREDIBLE... TO THINK HE COULD TAKE SUCH A BEATING AND STILL STAND -J-

WILL HONOR HIM... WITH A WARRIOR'S DEATH

SKILL AMPLIFICATION!! -J-

GET IN THE WAY...? WHAT DO YOU MEAN? GET IN THE WAY!

IT'S AS I SAID... OUR ROLE IN THIS BATTLE HAS ALREADY CONCLUDED... WE ARE NO LONGER NEEDED... AT LEAST FOR RIGHT NOW... ANYWAY

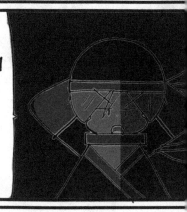

THEN TELL ME... WHY DID WE SPEND ALL OF THOSE YEARS TRAINING? WAS IT NOT FOR THIS BATTLE!? OR WERE YOU JUST WASTING OUR TIME?!

LISTEN... I UNDERSTAND WHERE YOU'RE COMING FROM... BUT THIS ORDER CAME FROM HIRO... SO IT'S OUT OF MY HANDS

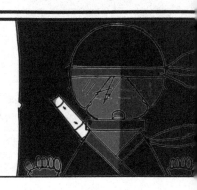

COME... EMBRACE
YOUR DARKNESS
-?-

IT'S DO OR DIE... YOU
OR HIM
-?-

SO, WHAT'S IT
GONNA BE?
-?-

THANKS FOR READING!...

...AND LOOK OUT FOR!

WELCOME
TO
PHANTOM
FALLS NO. 6 & 7

COMING IN 2026!